A NEW ORLEANS COMEDY

By Robert Williams

1

EXT. DECATUR STREET. JACKSON SQUARE. FRENCH
QUARTER. NEW ORLEANS. DUSK.

The streets are busy with throngs of tourists and early evening
revelers. It's the Mardi-Gras season and this part of the French
Quarter is noted for its mule drawn carriages, pavement artists,
and street performers plying their trade. A silver metallic robot
clown is packing up for the day and checking his takings, which
have been deposited in a cardboard box set in front of his pitch.
He smiles for the first time in 24 hours while counting his stash
- $152, not bad for a hard day's inactivity, punctuated by the
occasional Moon Walk.

In the fading light he sets off at a brisk pace down St. Peter
Street, heading in the direction of Louis Armstrong Park.

The metallic robot clown has to see a man about some heroin –
the silver routine pays for his brown.

Rear camera shot of the clown (as if he is being followed)
making his way towards the park. As he walks there are fewer
and fewer people on the street, until he is the sole pedestrian.
The shot fades to black.

EXT. SWAMP LAND. JEFFERSON PARISH. WEST OF NEW ORLEANS.

The body of a metallic robot clown is lying face up on a swamp bank, next to a waterway. The area has been cordoned off with police incident tape. Two detectives are stood over the body, while other police officers are sat in police dinghies and on swamp barges near to the scene.

Detective Kavanagh, a tough looking cop of Irish extraction and NOPD veteran, is the first to speak.

KAVANAGH

So, who found the body, Rancourt?

Kavanagh always addressed his colleague using his surname. Rancourt was a shorter, though stockier man, of French descent. Rene Rancourt could trace his New Orleans roots back 300 years. Though they had a healthy mutual respect for each other as police officers, there was no love lost between the two men - they mixed like beer and wine.

RANCOURT

The kid sat in the barge over there.

Rancourt points to a young man, aged 25 or thereabouts, sat on one of the nearby barges.

RANCOURT

He goes by the name of Captain Jason, and runs local swamp tours.

Pause.

RANCOURT

Says he was out on a barge doing his morning rounds checking on the local gators, prior to the first tourists showing up. He found the body at 7-15AM – a couple of gators were already chewing away at his right leg. It was the activity of the gators and the silver paint reflecting in the sun that caught his eye. Kavanagh nodded his assent; a sign Rancourt took as "pray continue".

RANCOURT

He wasn't sure if the body was real or not. Thought it might be some local kids playing a joke on him.

Pause.

RANCOURT

When he got close up and saw those gators chewing away at robot man here's flesh, he sped back to the lodge and called 911. The local sheriff was first on the scene. It seems clown homicide is now our specialty.

KAVANAGH

Well, it sure isn't suicide – otherwise there would be a boat here. There's no way to get to this spot by road.

Kavanagh looks around at the hostile swamp terrain.

KAVANAGH

Make sure the local cops scour the area for any boat that may have been used to ferry our man here.

RANCOURT

I'm already on it Lieutenant.

4

KAVANAGH

It sure makes a change from murdered hookers working out of Algiers.

Pause.

KAVANAGH

Silly question, but does anyone know who he is?

RANCOURT

So far, no. There was no I.D. found on him. I don't know about you, but these metallic robot clowns all look the same to me.

Rancourt smiles. Kavanagh doesn't return the smile.

KAVANAGH

I think we can say we are looking for at least one male perpetrator, familiar with the area, and with boats, that had a serious grudge against this particular clown.

Pause.

RANCOURT

Maybe he/they didn't find him funny?

Kavanagh is deep in thought and doesn't respond to his partner's quip.

KAVANAGH

Okay, once you've got Captain Jason's statement and had a chat with the locals, meet me back at Chartres Street. We need to get an autopsy on this clown fast.

Kavanagh smiles. Rancourt doesn't smile back. Touche.

KAVANAGH

Before the gators chew him all up.

Pause.

Shot of a gator scuttling off a nearby log into the water.

KAVANAGH

Where's the coroner?

RANCOURT

Doc Benoit is on his way.

KAVANAGH

He'll love this crime scene – it will appeal to his sense of the dramatic. Give him my regards.

Kavanagh climbs on to a police dinghy.

KAVANAGH (CONT'D)

If you're back at Chartres before me, make a start setting up an incident room. And phone me when the Doc is ready to start slicing up what's left of our friend here.

RANCOURT

Where you going now, Irishman?

KAVANAGH

I'm heading back to the French Quarter, to talk to a few clowns.

This time both men smile.

EXT.CHARTRES ST. FRENCH QUARTER POLICE STATION. NOON.

Kavanagh parks his unmarked outside the station, not even pausing to lock it. He slowly ambles off in the direction of the St. Louis Cathedral; a middle aged white dude in a crumpled suit, just blending in with the tourists.

Face on shot of Kavanagh as he unhurriedly negotiates the flow of human traffic (tourists and hustlers trying to lure clients into skin joints and 3 for 1 bars).

KAVANAGH V/O

I've lived in this city most of my life, ever since my folks moved down here from Chicago in the '70's.

Kavanagh lights himself a cigarette while barely breaking stride.

KAVANAGH V/O

I know all the whores and their pimps, the dealers and the users. Transients come and go but once this place gets into your blood, you become part of the fabric – a permanent fixture.

Pause.

A huge black doorman nods to Kavanagh, who reciprocates the gesture.

KAVANAGH V/O

I know the muggers and the pickpockets, the bar owners and the local drunks.

Kavanagh pauses at the junction with Toulouse St, as a mule drawn carriage carrying tourists high steps by.

KAVANAGH V/O

The street performers only come to my attention if they prove to be a nuisance. That being said, I like to study the faces behind the clown paint to see if they look familiar. A guy on the run, perhaps? Maybe a known pedophile trying to get close to kids?

Pause.

KAVANAGH V/O (CONT'D)

Your average street performer is usually a work shy bum looking for an easy buck, to feed a dope or a booze habit. So why would someone go to the trouble of murdering a two bit nothing and dumping him in the swamps 20 miles west of the Quarter? - unless the guy was a big fish laying low behind the clown persona?

Rancourt was right – metallic clowns *do* all look the same.

Kavanagh arrives at the Cathedral and takes a right through Jackson Square. He sees a metallic robot clown and heads straight for him.

Shot of Kavanagh stood in front of the metallic clown, who is motionless. Kavanagh flashes his NOPD badge at the clown who remains frozen.

KAVANAGH

Look buddy, you can cut the crap now. This is police business and I need to speak to you for a moment.

The clown remains dead still and silent. Kavanagh is getting visibly irritated by the clown's inertia but is reluctant to handle the clown for fear of the silver paint rubbing off on his hands.

A scruffy looking black guy comes running over to Kavanagh.

SCRUFFY DUDE

Hey man, cool it. You are talking to a real statue. That ain't no street performer. He belong to me.

Kavanagh looks puzzled.

SCRUFFY DUDE

I sit over there.

The scruffy dude points to a bar over the street.

SCRUFFY DUDE

When somebody put some money in the cup, I run over and collect. The statue belongs to me. I bring him here every day.

Kavanagh bursts out laughing.

KAVANAGH

Jeez, that's a new one. Even the human statues are fake these days. I should bust your ass for obtaining money by deception.

SCRUFFY DUDE

Aw, come on man. I'm just trying to turn a buck.

KAVANAGH

I'll let it go this once, but I need some information.

SCRUFFY DUDE

Anything you say bro.

KAVANAGH

As a metallic clown impersonator you must know the genuine article when you see it?

SCRUFFY DUDE

I make it my business to know, sure.

KAVANAGH

How many metallic clowns are working the Quarter right know? I'll narrow it down. How many *silver* metallic robot clowns are working in this area, to your knowledge?

As the scruffy dude is pondering this question a tourist pops a dollar into the pseudo-clown's cup.

KAVANAGH

Freaking unbelievable! - I can see I'm in the wrong business.

Scruffy dude smiles sheepishly. He is not completely devoid of a sense of shame, though he comes pretty close.

SCRUFFY DUDE.

Let me see. You mean *real* people posing as silver clowns?

KAVANAGH

Yeah, let's just stick with real people for now.

SCRUFFY DUDE

Well, there's Macca and Scotch Billy....and Alex that I know of.

KAVANAGH

Have you seen any of these characters today?

SCRUFFY DUDE

I saw Alex this morning because we shared a joint back at his place in Treme and Macca is on the other side of the Square.

Scruffy dude points at a metallic clown 200 yards away.

KAVANAGH

Are you sure he's not another statue?

Kavanagh can't hide the sarcasm in his tone.

SCRUFFY DUDE

Naw, that's him alright. He just moved. Look.

Scruffy Dude points at Macca but, when Kavanagh turns to look, Macca is motionless again. Kavanagh wearily shakes his head in frustration and takes a deep breath.

10

KAVANAGH

So you've seen both Alex and Macca today? What about
Scotch Billy?

SCRUFFY DUDE

Now you mention it, it's odd for him to not be here by now.

KAVANAGH

Why's that? Is he a particularly conscientious clown?

Scruffy Dude looks puzzled.

KAVANAGH

Is he always here at this time?

SCRUFFY DUDE

He sure is.

KAVANAGH

Why is he always here?

SCRUFFY DUDE

It ain't no secret man. Scotch Billy got one bad heroin habit. He
gotta pay the man somehow.

KAVANAGH

By "the man", are you talking generally or do you have
someone specific in mind?

SCRUFFY DUDE

I don't know no dealers, man. I don't know nothing. Booze is
my thing – always has been. That's why I do this fake clown
shit.

Kavanagh appears to accept his story. Nevertheless, he takes a $10 bill from his pocket and throws it in Scruffy Dude's collection box.

KAVANAGH

Is Scotch Billy of medium height and build, aged about 40?

SCRUFFY DUDE

Yeah man, that's him. Has anything happened to him? That sucker owes *me* $10.

KAVANAGH

Do you know where Scotch Billy lives?

SCRUFFY DUDE

He's homeless, man. Sometimes he gets a spot on some dude's floor but most of the time he's out on the street.

KAVANAGH

What's with the name Scotch Billy? Has he a surname?

SCRUFFY DUDE

It ain't his drink of choice if that's what you're thinking. Don't know no surname - he's a foreigner. I can't understand him most of the time. I think he's from Scotland. Ask Macca.

KAVANAGH

I think I might just do that. Thanks for your valuable time.

Scruffy Dude empties his collection box before returning to his bar stool over the road.

Kavanagh glances over at the metallic robot clown 200 yards away, who is moving in a robotic manner.

Kavanagh's phone rings - it's Rancourt.

12

KAVANAGH

Yep, Kavanagh.

RANCOURT

Rancourt here.

Doc Benoit has started the autopsy – he's requested our company ASAP. He wouldn't say anything specific over the phone but I can tell from his manner that there's something unusual about this case.

KAVANAGH

Yeah? It's beginning to grab my attention too.

Pause.

KAVANAGH

I have a possible victim I.D. – run a "Scotch Billy through the police computer against local drug misdemeanors in the last 12 months. We know he's about 40 years old and of medium height and build. Try the name "William" if nothing comes up for "Billy". I've no surname at this stage. Any possibles, print off the mug shots – we'll compare holiday snaps with the victim down at the city morgue. I'll meet you there within the hour. First I'm going to meet my third metallic robot clown of the day. Hopefully this one will talk.

RANCOURT

What's that?

KAVANAGH

Don't worry, I'm joking. I'll explain the joke to you later.

INT. AUTOPSY ROOM. CITY MORGUE. NEW ORLEANS.
2PM.

A body is laid out on an aluminum examination table. The skin of the cadaver has been peeled back to the waist, exposing the rib cage and internal organs.

Doc Benoit is examining the body while Kavanagh and Rancourt look on. A technician is seated in the corner of the room.

Doc Benoit is aged about 60, overweight, and wearing half moon spectacles, which he has a tendency to peer over when pontificating. The technician (Lesley) is a seedy looking middle aged cove.

DOC BENOIT

I hope you don't mind Kavanagh, but I started without you. Mr Rancourt stressed the urgency of this case, back in the swamp.

Rancourt nods his assent.

DOC BENOIT

Lesley, can you show the detectives the photographs of the deceased?

The technician gets off his chair and walks over to the detectives. He hands them a set of photographs of the victim's face pre-autopsy.

DOC BENOIT

Remind you of anyone?

I took the liberty of wiping off the silver face paint, samples of which have been sent off for analysis.

14

RANCOURT

William Rippey, aged 45, born Glasgow, Scotland, aka "Scotch Billy".

KAVANAGH

There's going to be one unhappy black dude down the Quarter – Scotch Billy owed him $10.

Pause.

KAVANAGH

Cause of death, Doc?

DOC BENOIT

He was struck with a heavy blunt instrument at the back of the skull, which caused a hairline fracture, but that didn't kill him.

Pause.

DOC BENOIT

In my opinion, "Scotch Billy" died from a massive heroin overdose.

KAVANAGH

That figures – he was a known addict.

DOC BENOIT

But this time his daily fix was not self administered. He received his fatal injection after he was rendered unconscious from a blow to the head.

KAVANAGH

Where was he injected?

DOC BENOIT

I've been saving this bit until you arrived. Lesley spotted it
straight away. I don't know what that says about Lesley.

Lesley laughs out loud from his seat in the corner of the room.

Doc begins to extract an object from the victim's rectum. It is an
empty syringe with a trace of brown viscous fluid in the
chamber.

DOC BENOIT

Voila !

Doc holds the syringe up to the light.

We are still waiting for the results of the blood works but I would
wager the contents of this syringe killed our man. It looks
likeScotch Billy died of a massive heroin overdose. Complete
shutdown of the central nervous system would be my verdict.

KAVANAGH

Somebody went to a lot of trouble to bludgeon this guy and
then give him enough heroin to kill him – that doesn't come
cheap. This guy would have had a high tolerance level after
years of addiction.

RANCOURT

I've assigned a couple of officers to ask around the usual junkie
hang out places.

KAVANAGH

Good. But I also think we need to send a couple of uniforms
down to Louis Armstrong Park. Get them to clear the park
around the "shooting gallery" area. You know where I mean?

RANCOURT

I'm on it.

KAVANAGH

Maybe Scotch Billy got attacked there. It's a long shot but there might be a patch of his blood or some other forensic clues.

Pause.

KAVANAGH

Our killer or killers went to a lot of trouble to "off" our friend here. He/they could have hidden the body, but it was left on display in a place where it would be found – a place that was difficult to get to.

RANCOURT

He/they, are making a statement.

KAVANAGH

Oh, it's a statement alright.

Thanks Doc. If you find anything else let me know straight away. As soon as the bloods confirm cause of death can you ring in?

DOC BENOIT

No problem Lieutenant.

The detectives start to leave the room.

KAVANAGH

What you eating for lunch today, Lesley?

LESLEY

I figured I'd have me a Beef Po Boy – all that juicy gravy running down my chin.

Lesley smiles and licks his fingers in a theatrically over the top way.

KAVANAGH

You are one sick puppy, Lesley.

LESLEY

Yes sir – that's me.

INT. INCIDENT ROOM. POLICE STATION. FRENCH QUARTER. 5PM.

Kavanagh and Rancourt are stood in front of a white board on which are tacked photos of the victim and swamp area where he was found. The name "Scotch Billy" and his known details are written on the board. Kavanagh is addressing a dozen or so police officers seated in the room.

KAVANAGH

Okay, gentlemen if I can have your attention.

To recap what we have so far.

Kavanagh half turns to point at the white board.

Victim, William Rippey, aged 45, born Glasgow Scotland 15th June 1965. No I.D. found on him but identified from police mug shots and records – 3 misdemeanors in New Orleans for drug related offences spaced out over an 18 month period; possession of a small amount of cannabis, possession of drug paraphernalia, and smoking hash in a public place.

Pause.

18

KAVANAGH (CONT'D)

Police in Scotland have been notified and are in the process of informing any living relatives and have promised to get back to us with any information they can unearth regarding William Rippey. That's RIPPEY, not RIPLEY.

Pause.

Kavanagh takes a sip from a cup of coffee. He makes a grimace.

KAVANAGH (CONT'D)

According to Customs and Immigration he entered the country via New York, 2 years ago, on a temporary visa and decided to illegally extend his stay. We know from his arrest record that he has been in the New Orleans area for at least 18 months.

An officer raises his hand – Officer Joyce, a fresh faced rookie, who is still keen as mustard.

JOYCE

Sir, why wasn't "Scotch Billy" deported after he came to the attention of the NOPD? He was technically an illegal immigrant.

KAVANAGH

I've no idea, Joyce. If you can think of an answer, I suggest you mail it express delivery to the President.

There is some laughter in the room.

KAVANAGH (CONT'D)

It seems he slipped through the net somehow. Put it down to bureaucratic failure.

KAVANAGH (CONT'D)

I'm not trying to fob you off Joyce, but if we could get back to the matter at hand.

Pause.

KAVANAH (CONT'D)

 Scotch Billy appears to be a known character on the streets of the Quarter thus supporting the notion that he has spent an extended period of time living in our beloved city.

Pause.

KAVANAGH (CONT'D)

 In recent months he has been working as a street performer – donning the guise of a silver metallic robot clown. We've all seen them working around Jackson Square and on Bourbon Street.

Kavanagh takes another sip of his coffee.

KAVANAGH (CONT'D)

An autopsy has revealed that the cause of death was a massive heroin overdose, administered by another party or parties when the victim was lying unconscious. Billy was knocked out cold by a heavy blunt instrument. We do not know where he was attacked.

Pause.

KAVANAGH (CONT'D)

Gentlemen, this is a murder inquiry. So let's keep the clown jokes down to a minimum. Scotch Billy was a loser, by all accounts, but we need to find his killer or killers.

Pause.

KAVANAGH (CONT'D)

 Doc Benoit estimates the time of death to be around midnight last night or the early hours of this morning. A tour guide called Captain Jason found the body in the swamp and phoned the local police in Jefferson Parish at 7-15am this morning. Detective Rancourt and I visited the crime scene 2 hours after the initial 911.

The body was dumped on a swamp bank, only accessible by boat, and left there for gator food. No attempt was made to conceal the body suggesting that the murderer or murderers wanted the body to be found.

Pause.

KAVANAGH (CONT'D)

 The location and positioning of the body indicate that the murderer or murderers are making a statement. We do not know as yet, what that statement is.

Pause.

KAVANAGH (CONT'D)

We are looking for one man or more who are organized and not acting on impulse, with physical strength, a cognizance of the New Orleans area, with financial means, access to a boat, and a grudge against William Rippey aka "Scotch Billy". Have you anything to add, Rancourt?

Kavanagh turns to his colleague.

RANCOURT

Captain Jason, who found the body, is clean. He has never been in trouble with the police – not even a speeding ticket. No abandoned boat, barge or raft has been found within a five mile radius of the crime scene, suggesting the "perp" or "perps" brought their own dinghy or small boat attached to a car. Nobody in the area reports seeing any suspicious activity in the area, in the early hours of this morning.

Pause.

RANCOURT (CONT'D)

Forensics from the swamp crime scene and the body have thus far produced no leads.

Pause.

RANCOURT (CONT'D)

All known junkie hangouts in the NO area have been searched for a possible heavy blunt weapon or for traces of fresh blood. So far, nothing has been turned up though the search by uniformed officers is ongoing as we speak. I want officers present here to divide up the tasks involved in trying to build up a comprehensive profile of Scotch Billy, his friends, associates, dealer, and fellow junkies. Does he have any enemies? Has he upset the wrong person? Did he aggravate one of the big players in town?

Pause.

22

RANCOURT (CONT'D)

You all know which bars to go in and who to start asking. I won't patronize you by naming names. In any event you may know people unknown to me and Lieutenant Kavanagh. Try and surprise us!

Pause.

RANCOURT (CONT'D)

We also need to get as clear a picture as possible of his last known whereabouts and movements. He was known to work out of Jackson Square and pack up for the day around 6/7PM. Talk to the other clowns and pavement artists as well as the carriage drivers.

Pause.

KAVANAGH

Okay gentlemen, I'm relying on you to come up with a lead. Unless, anyone has something to add, I suggest we hit the streets and gather as much information, pertaining to "Scotch Billy", as we can. Joyce raises a hand again.

KAVANAGH

Yes, Joyce?

JOYCE

What about the silver paint, sir? Was there anything distinctive about it?

Kavanagh turns to Rancourt.

RANCOURT

Good question, but unfortunately the paint *is* very common and can be bought at any fancy dress store or by mail order.

Besides, we now *know* the victim.

One or two of the officers snigger at the apparently pointless question.

JOYCE

I just wondered if it came off when you touched it, sir. Might not the killer have traces of the paint about their person?

RANCOURT

From what I've been told it doesn't come off when you touch it, and can be easily washed off the skin with soap and water. I don't think we will be able to spot the killer or killers walking round the French Quarter with tell tale silver hands.

One or two officers snigger again.

RANCOURT

But, another good question, Joyce. All this is new to me too.

Rancourt flashes a glare at the sniggering officers.

KAVANAGH

Okay, if there are no more questions, I suggest we go to work.

None of the other officers present has any questions. The meeting comes to a close and officers begin to file from the room.

24

INT. KAVANAGH'S APARTMENT. 4AM NEXT DAY.

The room is dark. Kavanagh is asleep in bed, alone. The phone rings. Kavanagh switches the bedside lamp on and wearily picks up his mobile phone.

KAVANAGH

Kavanagh – this better be good.

RANCOURT

Rancourt here. We've got ourselves another dead clown – The Super Dome, Poydres entrance.

KAVANAGH

What? Another silver robot clown?

RANCOURT

No. This one's a gold painted cowboy. He was found hanging from a street light, 30 minutes ago. I'm at the scene now - the area is cordoned off. I'll contact the Doc.

KAVANAGH

Okay, I'm on my way.

EXT. POYDRES STREET. THE SUPER DOME. NEW ORLEANS.

Shot of the gold painted Super Dome. In the foreground is a street lamp, from which hangs a gold painted cowboy; a rope tethered round his neck. He is lifeless. The area around the body is cordoned off. There are several police cars, complete with flashing lights, in attendance at the scene. The two detectives are stood in front of the body, looking up at the clown's face.

KAVANAGH

It looks like we've got ourselves a clown killer, with a sense of the dramatic.

Pause.

KAVANAGH (CONT'D)

Nobody saw anything suspicious, right?

RANCOURT

Nobody has come forward so far. A taxi driver was driving past and the body caught his eye. He thought it was a prank at first. Then, when he got a closer look he got spooked and phoned 911, just after 3-30AM.

KAVANAGH

His hands are tethered behind his back with cord. Maybe he was still alive when he was strung up?

Pause.

You say Doc Benoit is on his way?

RANCOURT

Yeah, I woke him up, and received a volley of abuse for my pains.

KAVANAGH

You were lucky you didn't get one from me, for good measure.

Pause.

KAVANAGH (CONT'D)

As soon as the Doc has seen him in situ; in the interest of decency we need to get him down as quickly as possible and get him back to the morgue. The crime scene forensic boys can take their time, but I want an autopsy on the cowboy as quickly as possible. Moreover, we won't know if he's carrying ID until we cut him down.

RANCOURT

I've organized some step ladders. Just waiting on the Doc.

KAVANAGH

Why would someone start whacking clowns?

Pause.

RANCOURT

I've heard of clown serial killers. Remember that guy, Gacy? He used the clown act to get close to kids, who he abducted, raped and murdered.

KAVANAGH

Yeah, I do. But I can't recall anyone wiping out clowns. What's the motive here?

RANCOURT

Maybe, it's someone who was abused by a clown and is now wreaking their revenge on *all* clowns?

KAVANAGH

Go on - I love it when you talk bullshit. William Rippey had no record of child molestation or pedophilia. The Scottish police said he had been arrested for shop lifting and minor drug offences. I'm surprised Joyce isn't here to ask how the hell he got in the US with a narcotics misdemeanor.

Both Kavanagh and Rancourt smile.

RANCOURT

Maybe the killer is a clown himself, and is wiping out the competition? Let's face it, there are too many of these assholes in the city.

KAVANAGH

Yeah, how's an honest clown expected to make a decent living?

Pause.

KAVANAGH (CONT'D)

Joking aside, there's a problem with that theory.

RANCOURT

What's that?

KAVANAGH

Our perp/perps have resources. We're talking a car, a boat, and money for drugs. Jeez, the killer even brings his own step ladders.

INT. AUTOPSY ROOM. CITY MORGUE. NEW ORLEANS. 10AM.

Doc Benoit is examining the body of the gold painted cowboy, which is laid out on the examining table. Kavanagh and Rancourt are in attendance. Lesley, the technician, is again seated on a chair in the corner of the room – he is picking his nose and eating the boogies.

KAVANAGH

Okay Doc, we know the ID of the victim - he was carrying his
social security card. The killer/killers saved us a bit of time, this
time round.

RANCOURT

The victim is a Nigel de Jong from Little Rock, Arkansas. A year
ago he walked out on his wife of 15 years and 3 kids, and a
steady job working on the railway. It seems he headed for New
Orleans. The last 3 months he has been claiming
unemployment benefits and must have taken up the clowning
to supplement his income with some tax free dollars.

KAVANAGH

Another bum, in other words. Only this time we're talking home
produced talent.

Pause.

KAVANAGH (CONT'D)

Unless I'm missing something, our victims, Rippey and de
Jong, appear to have nothing in common, apart from both being
in the clown business.

Doc Benoit nods as if in agreement with Kavanagh's words.

DOC BENOIT

De Jong here is a well built individual and does not possess the
usual drug addict physiognomy. Aside from not looking like a
drug abuser, there are no track marks on his arms or needle
holes. The results of the blood works confirm that Mr de Jong

had no illicit narcotic substances in his system at the time of his death.

KAVANAGH

What killed him Doc, if that's not an obvious question?

DOC BENOIT

It is not an obvious question, Lieutenant.

KAVANAGH

You mean he didn't die from hanging?

The Doc and Kavanagh enjoyed their Socratic style dialogues.

DOC BENOIT

That is correct.

KAVANAGH

Not another case of AIDS?

DOC BENOIT

AIDS?

Doc Benoit looks momentarily puzzled.

KAVANAGH

Ass Injected Death Sentence!

DOC BENOIT

Oh very droll detective.

LESLEY

Very witty Lieutenant. I'll have to remember that one for the guys in the canteen.

KAVANAGH

Okay, so we've established I'm wasting my talents and should be a standup comedian.

RANCOURT

Some think you already are, Kavanagh.

KAVANAGH

Steady, Frenchie. Don't forget I outrank you.

RANCOURT

I did say *some* think of you that way, present company excepted.

Kavanagh smiles sardonically.

KAVANAGH

Okay Doc, how did our victim die?

DOC BENOIT

He was first struck on the back of the head rendering him unconscious- the same MO as William Rippey - and then *strangled* with a rope.

PAUSE

DOC BENOIT (CONT'D)

Nigel de Jong died from asphyxiation. Several hours after his death, he was strung up from the street light which subsequently broke his neck. Strangulation rather than hanging caused our victim's death.

KAVANAGH

Can you give me a time of death?

DOC BENOIT

I would approximate the time of death as between 8 and 10pm last night.

KAVANAGH

So we are probably talking 5 or 6 hours between death and the stringing up of the body?

DOC BENOIT

I think we are talking that kind of time scale, yes.

RANCOURT

So the hanging is purely for theatrical purposes.

KAVANAGH

Absolutely. The killer or killers are sending the world a message.

LESLEY

So why are de Jong's hands tied behind his back if he was already dead when they hung him up?

KAVANAGH

You're not as dumb as you look Lesley boy.

LESLEY

I'll take that as a compliment detective.

Pause.

LESLEY (CONT'D)

Through years of watching the Doc, I've become a bit of a sleuth myself. The hand ties didn't make sense.

RANCOURT

If you wanted to hang someone you would tie their hands behind their back.

KAVANAGH

But the killer knew we would identify the true cause of death as strangulation.

RANCOURT

So we are being played?

KAVANAGH

Absolutely.

Pause.

KAVANAGH

The deaths are symbolic. The first victim was a junkie and killed by a lethal overdose; the second victim was killed by strangulation, but hung with his own cowboy rope – a gold painted clown displayed in front of a huge gold building.

Pause.

KAVANAGH (CONT'D)

There is also a playful element to these murders - the lethal syringe hidden up Rippey's ass; the simulated hanging of de Jong, with the misleading restraint of the hands. No ID on Scotch Billy's body; ID left on de Jong.

RANCOURT

Bludgeoning the victims with the heavy weapon is probably a necessary expedient. Once the victim is unconscious then a more dramatic death can be fashioned.

33

KAVANAGH

I agree. Strangulation was probably a necessary means to an end. It would have been too difficult to hang a live victim without drawing too much attention.

RANCOURT

Theatrical display is important but not at the expense of getting caught in the act.

KAVANAGH

Exactly.

LESLEY

This killer dude is one sick mother.

KAVANAGH

Coming from you, that's saying something.

LESLEY

It takes one to know one.

Kavanagh smiles.

KAVANAGH

So what are you having for lunch today, Lesley?

LESLEY

I was thinking maybe a full English breakfast and a side offer of waffles covered in Maple. Mm mm. I can taste it already.

KAVANAGH

I've never known anyone eat like you Lesley.

LESLEY

It's the work Lieutenant – gives me one hell of an appetite.

EXT. BOURBON ST. FRENCH QUARTER. NEW ORLEANS.
6PM.

A white faced clown, wearing a black and white hooped t-shirt
and a black beret, is practicing his mime act in the street. A
small crowd has gathered to watch. Two fat redneck hecklers,
holding "Huge Ass" beers, are giving the clown a hard time.
The mime is simulating being locked in an invisible box – he is
pushing against its imaginary walls.

FAT HECKLER 1

Hey, you faggot son of a bitch, why don't you get a proper job?
The mime continues undistracted, but suddenly his facial
expression turns to extreme sadness, as if he is hurt by the
heckler's comment.

FAT HECKLER 2

That's it you pooh pusher – cry your freaking eyes out.
Some members of the crowd are laughing along with the
hecklers, but others are visibly uncomfortable with the tone of
the abuse. Suddenly the mime pulls a realistic gun from the
back of his trousers. The clown's face is now deadly serious.
He points the gun at the hecklers. The crowd goes quiet, not
sure whether the mime is serious or not.

FAT HECKLER 1

Hey man. We were just fooling around.

FAT HECKLER 2

That's not a real gun is it?

The hecklers have both turned ashen. Suddenly the clown pulls the trigger of the gun, and a bouquet of flowers springs from the barrel. The mime holds the flowers aloft and theatrically bows to the crowd. There is loud applause and a couple of people place dollar bills in the clown's cup. The hecklers have now regained their composure and start to move off up the street.

FAT HECKLER 1

I always knew the gun wasn't real.

FAT HECKLER 2

Me too. C'mon Hank, I fancy me another of these Huge Ass beers.

FAT HECKLER 1

Now you are talking. I've had enough of this clown shit for one day. I read in the local paper that someone has been bumping these assholes off.

FAT HECKLER 2

I'd sure like to buy that dude a drink.

FAT HECKLER

Amen to that brother.

The two fat hecklers walk away, leaving the mime artist to pick up his tips.

Close up shot of the clown's face. He looks murderous.

EXT. RIVERBOAT DOCKS. NEW ORLEANS. 8AM.

A riverboat is anchored by the docks. Several police cars have closed off the dockside area to the general public. There is the hubbub and police activity associated with a freshly discovered crime scene. An unmarked police car pulls up at the scene – Kavanagh and Rancourt get out. Detective Joyce greets them.

KAVANAGH

So what have we got, Joyce?

JOYCE

A jogger noticed the body at 6-30AM. Uniform arrived here at 6-46AM.

The three detectives walk to the river boat stern. A body is tied, in a crucifix position, to the paddle wheel. The victim is a seventies transvestite glam rock type: a heavily made up male wearing a gold *lame* dress and silver platform boots. There is heavy blood staining of the dress around the groin area of the body.

KAVANAGH

Another clown, or are we back to the usual hooker murder?

RANCOURT

Hard to say, Lieutenant. He certainly looks like a clown, with the gold and silver look.

JOYCE

I think he *was* a clown.

Kavanagh and Rancourt turn to look at Joyce.

KAVANAGH

What makes you say that, Joyce?

JOYCE

I think I have seen the victim working on Decatur Street.

Pause.

JOYCE

He stands motionless in empty doorways, as a transvestite metallic painted human statue.

RANCOURT

You sure?

JOYCE

Pretty much. I remember seeing him and thinking he was unusual because of the transvestite angle. That's how I remember him. He's the only transvestite human statue I've seen.

KAVANAGH

So it's official – we have ourselves a clown serial killer.

RANCOURT

Well done Joyce. At least we now know we are looking for the same killer.

KAVANAGH

Or killers.

RANCOURT

Serial killers usually work alone, but I take your point Lieutenant.

KAVANAGH

If we are talking one man, then this guy is seriously organized. He must have transported this victim by boat, in order to gain access to the paddle wheel.

RANCOURT

You're right. To tie someone to the wheel you would have to do it using a boat – there's no practicable access from the dock side. It fits with the MO of the Scotch Billy murder.

KAVANAGH

The papers are going to have a field day with this, now we are looking for a serial killer.

RANCOURT

Our man is getting what he wants – he craves publicity judging by the manner of the murders.

KAVANAGH

Talk about playing to the gallery.

JOYCE

Do you think our murderer wants to get caught, sir?

Joyce addresses Kavanagh.

KAVANAGH

Not yet, Joyce. I've a feeling he's only just started.

Pause.

KAVANAGH (CONT'D)

We've had gator infested swamps, The Super Dome, and now a Mississipi river boat. He's not exhausted all the potential New Orleans themes, by a long way.

RANCOURT

What's next? A clown found drowned in a vat of gumbo?

KAVANAGH

The way things are going, I wouldn't rule it out.

39

Pause.

KAVANAGH (CONT'D)

Joyce, I want you to follow up your I.D. of our victim here. Try and find out as much as possible about him, and his last known movements. Somebody must know him on Decatur Street.

Joyce nods.

Pause.

KAVANAGH

So what's your theory now, Rancourt?

RANCOURT

Our man has a serious problem with street performers. The big question is, why?

KAVANAGH

Brilliant! , Holmes.

RANCOURT

If you'll let me finish, Watson?

Rancourt smiles as does Kavanagh, begrudgingly.

RANCOURT (CONT'D)

We are assuming that the murderer has a motive. Maybe there is no motive. If a psychopath just wanted to get off by killing people randomly and avoid detection, then killing *clowns* would be the perfect victimology.

Pause.

KAVANAGH

Please develop your argument.

RANCOURT (CONT'D)

Firstly, no one really gives a shit about street clowns. Secondly, the bodies can lie around the city for hours before anyone notices that they have been murdered. People walk past lifeless clowns either thinking they *are* statues, or that the lifelessness is part of their act.

Pause.

RANCOURT (CONT'D)

Somebody fooling around with an inert looking clown in the early hours of the morning doesn't seem odd in this city, particularly during Mardi-Gras season. Because nothing looks odd in New Orleans, the killer can go about his business without attracting attention, and put time and distance between himself and the crime scene.

KAVANAGH

So you think these could be motiveless killings? The murderer is killing clowns because killing clowns is easy?

RANCOURT

No sir. I think our man has a serious grudge against the clowning fraternity.

Killing tramps and the homeless would be equally facile. The theatrical nature of the killings and the fact that he wants to make public displays of his victims, suggests he is making a statement about street clowns. He is motivated to murder and humiliate this group.

KAVANAGH

But why?

RANCOURT

I don't know Lieutenant. We need more clues.

Kavanagh turns to Joyce.

KAVANAGH

Do we know what caused the heavy blood stains on the dress?

Kavanagh points at the transvestite victim, still tied to the
paddle wheel.

JOYCE

I overheard the first officers on the scene say that the victim's
genitalia had been cut off.

INT. "BOB MARLEY" BAR. BOURBON STREET.

The bar is dimly lit to the point of complete darkness. A two
man reggae band is playing on a small stage. A young African
American barmaid is serving a solitary customer. The customer
is dressed as a Harlequin, in a diamond patterned costume with
his face blacked up. The bartender has lined him up three
bottles of beer.

BARMAID

Okay, that's $18 for three beers.

HARLEQUIN

Excuse me?

BARMAID

$18, buddy.

42

HARLEQUIN

It says 3 for 1 outside. So I owe you $6.

BARMAID

The type of beers you ordered are not part of the 3 for 1 offer.

HARLEQUIN

Bull shit. They were the other day.

BARMAID

That was the other day. This is now.

The barmaid is adopting a smart ass hostile attitude.

HARLEQUIN

I don't want them then. I'm not paying.

BARMAID

But I've opened them now. You have to pay.

HARLEQUIN

Whatever beer I would have ordered you would have said they weren't part of the 3 for 1 offer. Do you think I'm stupid? Either take the $6 for three or keep them.

BARMAID

So you're not paying?

Harlequin mouths the word "NO".

BARMAID (CONT'D)

Leroy!

The barmaid shouts for the huge Rastafarian bouncer to come over. He approaches the Harlequin in a menacing manner. Harlequin calmly picks up one of the bottles.

HARLEQUIN

So the beers are $18 – that's $6 each, right?

The barmaid nods. Harlequin suddenly smashes the bottle in the face of the bouncer who falls to the ground clutching his face in agony, blood pumping from his wounds. The reggae band stop playing, while the barmaid suddenly looks terrified. Harlequin slowly counts out $6 which he has taken from a pocket.

HARLEQUIN (CONT'D)

Here's $6. I only needed the *one* beer.

Harlequin casually steps over the body of the screaming bouncer and exits the bar.

INT. INCIDENT ROOM. POLICE STATION. FRENCH QUARTER. DAY.

Kavanagh and Rancourt are stood at the front of the Incident Room, facing the assembled murder investigation team, consisting of a dozen or so seated detectives, including the rookie Joyce.

KAVANAGH

If I could have your attention please, gentlemen.

Pause.

The room comes to a hushed silence.

KAVANAGH (CONT'D)

It's official – we are now looking for a clown serial killer.

There is some murmuring in the room. Kavanagh raises the volume of his voice a notch.

44

KAVANAGH (CONT'D)

First victim, William Rippey aka Scotch Billy, found dead in the swamp. Cause of death massive heroin overdose, fatally administered by our killer or killers.

Pause.

KAVANAGH (CONT'D)

The FBI experts in Quantico have been studying this case and are now working with the NOPD in an advisory capacity.

Murmuring in the room.

KAVANAGH (CONT"D)

I know, I know….but until informed otherwise NOPD is still handling the case and I am in charge of this investigation.

Pause.

KAVANAGH (CONT'D)

Their current thinking, based on past serial killer cases with a similar MO, though frankly there's never been anything quite like this, is that we are more than likely looking for a single killer.

Pause.

KAVANAGH (CONT'D)

More than likely is the key phrase here. We will pursue this investigation on the basis that we are looking for a lone killer, but not totally rule out the possibility that he may have an accomplice.

KAVANAGH (CONT'D)

The fact that we are looking for a *lone wolf* killer, does not make our job of finding him any easier. If anything, the organization involved in the commission of these murders and his ability to avoid detection thus far, suggests we are dealing with a highly intelligent, organized and motivated individual.
Pause.

KAVANAGH (CONT'D)

Serial killers usually murder within their own racial group and tend to be males. Given the heavy physical nature of hauling and lifting bodies – de Jong was a particularly heavy man – I think we can safely say we are looking for a male killer.
Pause.

KAVANAGH (CONT'D)

The fact that he is calculating and has financial means, points to him being a mature man aged between 30 and 50 years of age. It's likely that he has murdered before or committed acts of violence. In summary, we are looking for a white male, aged 30-50, with at least one felony for violence.
Pause.

KAVANAGH (CONT'D)

I know there are thousands of guys who fit that description in New Orleans alone, but at least it's a start in narrowing down our search. I've already assigned a couple of officers to work through computer records of known felons who fit the criteria – the FBI is doing the same.

Kavanagh points to the photo of the second victim, taped to the white board.

KAVANAGH (CONT'D)

Our second victim, Nigel de Jong from Little Rock Arkansas. A gold cowboy found hanging outside the Super Dome – cause of death strangulation. Street clowning appears to be the only common trait shared by Rippey and de Jong. Which brings me to our third victim, and credit must go to Detective Joyce for recognizing Thomas George aka, wait for it, "Rock-on-Tommy". Joyce acknowledges some good humored banter and applause from his fellow officers.

KAVANAGH (CONT'D)

George, aka Rock-on-Tommy, was found lashed to the paddle wheel of the Riverboat "Creole Queen". He died from extreme blood loss – his genitalia had been cut off with some kind of hunting knife.

A couple of the seated officers wince at this last piece of information.

KAVANAGH (CONT'D)

George was a transvestite miming clown who worked Decatur. He was a popular local character with no known enemies. Originally, George hailed from New York but told friends he liked it down here for the warm weather. The autopsy and forensic investigation have given us no leads thus far. Our killer is meticulous in covering his tracks. That sums up what we have so far —one big fat zero. Gentlemen, the floor is now yours

- has anyone got anything to add?

A detective raises his hand.

KAVANAGH (CONT'D)

Yes, Savard?

OFFICER SAVARD

Well sir, it may be nothing, but something one of my informers

told me the other day struck me as odd.

Pause.

KAVANAGH

Go on.

OFFICER SAVARD

It came from a black girl I busted last summer for boosting

tourists' credit cards, when she was working as a waitress in

the "Cajun Kabin". I went easy on her that time so she owes

me.

Pause.

OFFICER SAVARD (CONT'D)

She works as a bartender now in "Bob Marley's" bar.

KAVANAGH

That den of iniquity! She'll be right at home.

OFFICER SAVARD

She says she was working a couple of days ago and the

bouncer Leroy got glassed by a customer over a disputed bill.

But here's the funny thing – the attacker was dressed weird,

like a clown.

RANCOURT

I don't recall the incident being reported – I'd have noticed.

OFFICER SAVARD

That's because it wasn't reported. The "Bob Marley" is so heavy with cannabis fumes, I got the munchies when I walked in the place. They certainly don't want the NOPD dropping in for a social visit.

A couple of officers laugh.

OFFICER SAVARD

My source says the dude was dressed up in a costume that had a diamond pattern and his face was blacked up with face paint. She's positive the guy was white because she saw his hands.

JOYCE

The diamond pattern sounds like the Harlequin design. Harlequins were the clowns that preceded the white faced clowns we see today, and are sometimes portrayed with black faces.

KAVANAGH

Very interesting Joyce - how do you know all this?

JOYCE

I've been reading up on the history of clowning, sir.

RANCOURT

Could be nothing, or it could be significant. I was beginning to think that the killer may be dressed as a cop or someone in a position of trust. He seems to have no trouble initially meeting his victims. Now, prompted by Savard and Joyce's comment, I'm thinking he may be *another* clown. That would explain his ability to get up close to other clowns.

KAVANAGH

So you're saying we may be looking for a *killer clown* who's a *clown killer*? - an interesting theory, Rancourt.

RANCOURT

It's a possibility sir.

KAVANAGH

This case is getting weirder by the minute. Thanks for your input Savard, and your erudite contribution, Joyce.

Pause.

KAVANAGH (CONT'D)

I think we need to haul in this Harlequin character if only to eliminate him from our inquiry.

OFFICER SAVARD

We need to get to him before Leroy, the bouncer, and his friends, sir. The word is out on the streets and the Harlequin is history if they find him before we do.

RANCOURT

I'll inform uniform to keep an eye out for the Harlequin.

JOYCE

If you think it would help, I can download a picture of the Harlequin costume off the internet, and print up some pictures for general distribution round the station?

50

KAVANAGH

Good idea, Joyce. Are you after my job?

Shot of Joyce smiling and blushing.

RANCOURT

If we are looking for a killer clown, we are back to the theory that he may be wiping out the competition – the motive could be economic?

KAVANAGH

I don't buy it. We're missing something.

RANCOURT

Or maybe he dons the clown disguise so he can move freely around The Quarter without arousing any suspicion?

KAVANAGH

So the clown disguise is tactical? He's some right wing vigilante type cleaning the streets of New Orleans; hosing away the human trash?

Pause.

KAVANAGH (CONT'D)

Mm, if that's the case he may have to drop the clown disguise – the street performers have stopped working nights and some have gone back to straight begging.

RANCOURT

Looking like a tramp or a homeless person doesn't count as street performing - they should be safe in their civilian attire.

KAVANAGH

At this rate our killer will be the *only* clown in town.

Literally, but not figuratively speaking. Okay gentlemen, we are looking for a middle aged white male, moneyed, intelligent, strongly built, with a history of violence. And wait for it….. he may be dressed as a clown – a Harlequin no less.

INT. KILLER CLOWN'S APARTMENT. NEW ORLEANS.

The room is a shrine to comic greats from the past. The walls are festooned with posters of Chaplin, Buster Keaton, and lithographs of historic clowns such as Grimaldi and Marcel Marceau. There are mannequins sporting various clown costumes; various metallic outfits in silvers and golds.

Close up shot of a mannequin draped with a Harlequin outfit. Circus music is playing.

Shot of the killer clown sat at his dressing table. He is looking in the mirror, surrounded by light bulbs, while applying the finishing touches to his latest character creation – a tribute to Benny Hill; wire framed spectacles with cap worn askew.

Shot of the killer's face as he salutes the mirror, eyes blinking furiously, in the comic style of Benny Hill.

KILLER CLOWN

Good evening, viewers.

The clown speaks with the preposterous Hampshire burr of the English comic legend.

Shot fades to black.

INT. FLANAGAN'S BAR. FRENCH QUARTER. NIGHT.

Face on shot of Scruffy Dude sat at the bar. On the stool next to him is sat Scruffy Dude's metallic statue. Scruffy Dude is clearly drunk – he is trying to attract the barman's attention. The barman, a twenty something red headed Irish guy, has spotted Scruffy Dude's raised finger.

BARMAN

Another beer with a whiskey chaser?

SCRUFFY DUDE

That's me……..but don't get my friend one.

Scruffy Dude looks at his statue. The barman smiles wearily – it is the tenth time he's heard the same line that night. He serves the drinks but waits for Scruffy Dude to pay cash before moving off.

Shot fades to black.

Face on shot of Scruffy Dude slumped on the bar. Even his statue on the next seat has slumped face down on the bar. The barman starts to shake Scruffy Dude by the arm.

BARMAN

C'mon buddy. It's time to go home – I'm closing the bar.

SCRUFFY DUDE

What time is it man?

Scruffy Dude looks befuddled.

BARMAN

It's 4AM. Time you and your friend were leaving.

He nods at the statue. Scruffy Dude wearily slides off his stool and lifts up his statue, which is made of *papier mache* and therefore light in weight. He staggers out of the bar with the statue under his arm.

EXT.SAINT LOUIS NUMBER 1 CEMETERY. NEW ORLEANS.
DAWN.

Aerial shot of St Louis Number 1 Cemetery. The cemetery
entrance has been blocked off by several police cars with
flashing lights. Camera closes in on a particular tomb. Close up
shot of tomb – Scruffy Dude's lifeless body, which has been
sprayed with silver paint, is propped up in a seating position
against the tombstone. Scruffy Dude's statue is seated next to
the body in a similar pose. A bottle of whiskey is placed
between the body and the statue – they look as though they are
sharing a drink. Kavanagh and Rancourt are stood by the tomb,
inspecting the crime scene.

KAVANAGH

I met our victim and his dummy the other day, down at Jackson
Square. *He* wasn't sprayed with silver paint at the time.

Kavanagh points at Scruffy Dude.

RANCOURT

So this is the *fake* metallic clown operative you told me about?

KAVANAGH

Yeah, this is, or should I say *was* the guy.

Pause.

KAVANAGH (CONT'D)

In death, he is a *real* metallic clown for the first time.

RANCOURT

It looks like our killer was trying to give him a helping hand with
his career, by supplying the free paint job.

54

Shot of Scruffy Dude's silver painted face.

KAVANAGH

Yeah, the killer must have appreciated the performance.

Kavanagh points to a cardboard box at Scruffy Dude's feet containing a $20 bill.

KAVANAGH (CONT'D)

The guy was just a harmless drunken bum.

Aerial shot of Saint Louis Number 1 Cemetery. Shot fades to black.

EXT. BOURBON STREET.FRENCH QUARTER. NEW ORLEANS. AFTERNOON.

The killer is dressed as Jacques Tati's eccentric character, Monsieur Hulot; box trilby hat, ill fitting suit buttoned up, trousers too short, white socks with black loafers. "Hulot" has an unlit pipe in his mouth, completing the comic ensemble – he is walking on slightly exaggerated tiptoes. In a town full of eccentrics no one finds his appearance the least bit unusual. The killer is walking down the street in a completely carefree manner. Shot of "Hulot" stopping in the street, to peer into a shop window, evidently fascinated by the display of overpriced tourist kitsch. His actions constitute a finely crafted performance, which no one is aware of.

INT. CAFÉ. FRENCH QUARTER. NEW ORLEANS. LATE AFTERNOON.

The café interior is chic and Parisian inspired. Post Impressionist prints adorn the walls and there is a clean simplicity about the white table cloths, each set with a vase of freshly cut flowers. The waitresses are smartly dressed in white blouses with black skirts. There is the sound of clinking cups and spoons as the staff busily shuttle from kitchen to table. "Monsieur Hulot" has just arrived and is seated alone at a table by the window – he is contentedly reading his newspaper while sucking on his unlit pipe. A waitress approaches. She is in her thirties with average good looks – her hair is cut in a bob.

WAITRESS

Are you ready to order sir?

"Hulot" is startled and struggles to fold his newspaper into a manageable size before placing it on the table and looking up at the waitress. He raises his hat to the waitress.

"HULOT"

One moment, *mademoiselle*.

Hulot spies a hat stand on the other side of the room and walks over to it. Several café customers have to move their chairs in order for Hulot to reach the hat stand. He removes his hat and places it on the stand. He then returns to his table with a loping gait, and sits down before looking up at the waitress. The waitress is smiling – she is intrigued by the awkward stranger with his old world manners.

"HULOT"

May I?….mm.

Hulot is mumbling due to the pipe being in his mouth. He removes the pipe and places it on the table. The waitress finds it hard to suppress her laughter.

"HULOT"

May I 'ave a cup of tay, mademoiselle?

Hulot speaks with a French accent.

WAITRESS

Certainly, sir - anything else?

"HULOT"

No thank you – that eez all.

The waitress goes off to the kitchen to get Hulot his tea. Hulot is rummaging in his trouser pockets and pulls out a handful of coins. He drops one of the coins which rolls under the table of two well-to-do middle aged ladies, partaking of afternoon tea. Hulot gets down on his knees and attempts to retrieve the coin, much to the consternation of the two matrons. At one point Hulot crawls between the legs of one of the ladies, though his intentions are purely innocent. Hulot's performance causes quite a kerfuffle until finally he grabs the coin and returns to his seat with much bowing and apology making. The waitress returns with Hulot's tea, oblivious of the pantomime that has just taken place.

WAITRESS

Here you are, sir. One cup of tea.

"HULOT"

Thank you meez.

57

The waitress smiles at Hulot's absurd, though endearing, behavior.

WAITRESS

I hope you don't mind me asking, but are you French?

"HULOT"

Oui, Yes mademoiselle. I am from Paris.

WAITRESS

Wow. I've always wanted to visit Paris. It looks such a beautiful city.

"HULOT"

It eez very 'istoric. Maybe one day you will see eet.

WAITRESS

I hope so.

The waitress looks wistful.

WAITRESS (CONT'D)

Are you on holiday?

"HULOT"

Oui. I am on an extended vacation.

Hulot notices the waitresses name badge – "NANCY".

"HULOT" (CONT'D)

I am 'ere in New Orleans for 3 months, to see the Mardi-Gras – the "Fat Tuesday", Nancy.

The waitress blushes slightly at Hulot's use of her name.

WAITRESS

You noticed my name. What do I call you?

She smiles.

"HULOT"

Jacques. My name is Jacques.

The conversation leads to a slightly awkward silence. Hulot takes a sip of his tea. Some tea has spilled in the saucer. He pours the contents of the saucer into his cup with total concentration. Nancy smiles again. Hulot notices the smile and smiles back. Suddenly Hulot's attention is drawn to one of the paintings on the wall.

"HULOT"

Ze painting there….

Hulot points to one of the paintings.

"HULOT" (CONT'D)

It eez not hanging straight.

Hulot gets up and walks over to the painting, unlit pipe in mouth. He attempts to straighten the painting, which looked fine in the first place. Again, other customers in the café have had to move their chairs in order for Hulot to gain access to the picture. After several failed attempts at adjusting the painting, Hulot nods at the picture and returns to his seat. The painting is now hanging more crookedly than it was originally. Nancy smiles again at the odd French man.

WAITRESS/NANCY

You know, if you ever need a guide around New Orleans, I would be willing to show you the sites. Hulot smiles in a shy way.

"HULOT"

I would like that very much, mademoiselle.

INT. INCIDENT ROOM. POLICE HQ. FRENCH QUARTER.
NEW ORLEANS.

Kavanagh is addressing the murder investigation team. On the
white board are tagged the photos pertaining to the
investigation.

KAVANAGH

Gentlemen, it's been a week now since we found our fourth
victim, Denzil Williams –discovered dead in St Louis Number 1
cemetery.

Kavanagh points to a mug shot photo of Denzil Williams, aka
"Scruffy Dude".

KAVANAGH (CONT'D)

He died of acute alcohol poisoning. The last person to see him
alive was a barman in Flanagan's bar. He told police that Denzil
had left at closing time and was extremely drunk; but no more
inebriated than usual. The autopsy has revealed that Denzil
died of acute alcohol poisoning – his blood levels revealed that
he had consumed the equivalent of three bottles of spirits. Any
normal individual; even a hardened drinker like Denzil, would
have passed out after two bottles. It looks like our killer made
the victim drink himself to death, maybe at gunpoint? The
theatrical nature of the crime scene has our killer's signature all
over it.

KAVANAGH (CONT'D)

It seems our killer is taking a break from proceedings. Unless that is, we haven't found his fifth victim yet?

Pause.

KAVANAGH (CONT'D)

An unlikely possibility I think, given his previous *modus operandi*. He likes to leave his victims on public display, where they can be easily found.

Pause.

KAVANAGH (CONT'D)

So I think we can assume he has stopped for now, for whatever reason.

RANCOURT

Maybe he has stopped for good?

KAVANAGH

Let's hope so.

Pause.

KAVANAGH (CONT'D)

But let's work on the basis that he could start again any time. The fact that we haven't found a fifth victim yet, doesn't mean finding this maniac is any less urgent.

RANCOURT

Maybe he's waiting for the street clowns to start drifting back? Give it another week and the "clown killer" will be yesterday's news.

61

KAVANAGH

Yeah, that's what I'm afraid of.

Pause.

KAVANAGH (CONT'D)

Still been no sightings of our Harlequin?

RANCOURT

Nada, Lieutenant.

The room is silent. Then Joyce raises his hand.

JOYCE

Maybe we should be looking for another type of clown?

RANCOURT

There are no clowns in The Quarter right now. Take a look around – our killer has scared them all off.

KAVANAGH

But as you said – give it a week and they'll be back. I think Joyce is right. As soon as the clowns start coming out of the woodwork, let's start hauling them in for questioning – *all* of them.

Pause.

KAVANAGH (CONT'D)

So far, our investigation has produced nothing tangible. We need to be more proactive. As soon as anyone sees a metallic robot or Harlequin, grab him and haul his ass in for interrogation - say it's for his own safety, if he starts quoting the First, Fourth, or Fifth Amendments.

Pause.

KAVANAGH (CONT'D)

Okay men, get out on the street and bring me some clowns!
The meeting comes to an end and the officers file out of the
room.

EXT. PARISIAN CAFÉ. FRENCH QUARTER. NEW ORLEANS.

Shot of the café front. Nancy is waiting outside. "Hulot" pulls up
in an ancient Citroen motorcar. He alights from the driver's side
and walks round to the passenger side to open the door for
Nancy, bowing as he does so. They both get in the car which
starts to pull off with Hulot at the wheel – the car's exhaust
loudly backfires. A hundred yards down the road, they pass a
police van as a silver clown is being manhandled into the back
by two burly uniformed officers.

Camera follows Hulot's jalopy as it winds its way through the
narrow streets of the French Quarter, causing mayhem as it
does so. People are hurriedly jumping out of the way as Hulot
toots his horn and the old car repeatedly backfires.

Soundtrack: Django Reinhardt – Jazz Guitar – "I'll See You in
My Dreams".

Face on shot of Hulot at the steering wheel; Nancy by his side.
Hulot has an unlit pipe in his mouth and is wearing his usual rig
of box trilby, buttoned up suit, shirt and tie. Nancy is wearing a
summer frock.

Music fades.

INT. CITY AQUARIUM. NEW ORLEANS.

Soundtrack: Erik Satie – Piano Works – Gymnopedies, Lent et Douloureux.

Shot of Hulot and Nancy stood hand in hand in front of a giant fish tank – manta rays and sharks are languidly swimming.

EXT. PLANTATION MANSION. NEW ORLEANS. AFTERNOON.

Soundtrack of Erik Satie continues.

Shot of a classically designed, disused, plantation mansion. Nancy is stood in front of the house looking at its façade. Hulot keeps popping his head out of a different window, first top left, then 5 seconds later bottom right etc, much to the amusement of Nancy.

EXT. FRENCH QUARTER. NEW ORLEANS. LATE AFTERNOON.

Soundtrack of Erik Satie continues.

Hulot and Nancy approach a mule drawn carriage with a view to taking a tour of The Quarter. On seeing Hulot, the mule rears up on its hind legs. The carriage driver manages to calm the mule down, and Hulot and Nancy tentatively climb into the carriage. The mule sets off at a break neck pace.

Close up shot of Nancy laughing mutely – she is having the time of her life. Hulot smiles in a genuine, albeit reserved, manner.

EXT. RIVERSIDE. NEW ORLEANS. SUNSET.

Soundtrack of Erik Satie continues.

64

A romantic scene as Hulot and Nancy walk arm in arm along the river bank, as a steamboat gently glides past. The mood is only momentarily broken when a passer-by's dog goes for Hulot's leg; the cur being quickly restrained by its owner.

As the couple gaze lovingly at the fading sun, the music gently comes to an end.

INT. "THE BEACH" BAR. BOURBON STREET. FRENCH QUARTER. NEW ORLEANS. AFTERNOON.

Kavanagh and Rancourt are sat at the bar. Kavanagh is drinking Guinness, Rancourt a small glass of red wine. A group of noisy tourists are taking turns at bashing a boxing ball which records the force of one's punch. There is much hollering and banter as successive guys in the group take their turn. The two detectives are doing their best to ignore the commotion. There is a momentary lull as "Hulot's" car careers past the bar and backfires loudly. Neither detective realizes the significance of the clown car or its driver.

RANCOURT

If it's any consolation Lieutenant, I think you have done everything humanly possible to find the clown killer. He has stopped for now, but my gut instinct is that he'll kill again.

Kavanagh finishes his pint and raises his finger to the barman who starts to pour another.

RANCOURT (CONT'D)

I know you are pissed that the Mayor and the Chief have ordered you to release all the clowns.

65

The barman places the fresh pint in front of Kavanagh. He takes a drink.

RANCOURT (CONT'D)

We weren't getting anywhere with the jokers we hauled in. One even pleaded the right to silence using mime.

Rancourt puts his finger to his lips.

KAVANAGH

Yeah, that guy was too much. I felt like beating the shit out of him with the volume turned down.

RANCOURT

It's been a couple of weeks since the last murder. Now that the clowns are going to be free and on the streets, the killer may resurface.

KAVANAGH

Yeah, hopefully number five will be the 5th Amendment clown. That would be poetic justice.

Pause.

KAVANAGH (CONT'D)

You still think our killer is dressed as a clown?

RANCOURT

Not right now. We dragged in every clown in town – they were dead beats to a man and incapable of systematic thought. Our man has either left the city or is currently dressed normally.

Hulot's car drives past the bar, this time going in the opposite direction – it backfires noisily. Neither detective pays the car any heed.

The boxing ball group start hollering.

KAVANAGH

And you pricks can shut the fuck up!

A couple of the group start to glare at Kavanagh. Rancourt flashes his NOPD badge. The group of revelers stop glaring at Kavanagh and continue to amuse themselves with the boxing ball.

RANCOURT

They're just kids Lieutenant.

KAVANAGH

Yeah, I know. I've just got a low clown tolerance threshold right now.

Kavanagh takes a long swallow of his pint.

KAVANAGH (CONT'D)

Is there anything we've missed? Talk to me Rancourt.

RANCOURT

We've reviewed the case a thousand times. No physical clues have been found. The public appeal for information you made on TV has produced nothing. *We* need to establish a motive and why he has suddenly stopped killing.

Pause.

KAVANAGH

Keep going.

RANCOURT

The money motive has been ruled out - our killer is a man of means. The fact that he is killing *clowns* is significant, but we don't know why. The victims have all been bums without serious criminal records, so it doesn't look like revenge is the motive. If the killer is a vigilante cleaning the streets then why doesn't he kill the tramps and the homeless? There doesn't appear to be a sexual or racial motive. Our last victim, Denzil Williams, was black and aside from the first victim having a syringe rammed up his ass, there has been no violation of the victims.

KAVANAGH

The transvestite was violated – he had his dick and balls cut off.

RANCOURT

True. But there wasn't a sexual motive. He was a transvestite, so our killer gave him a crude sex change. The murder is symbolic rather than sexually motivated.

Pause.

RANCOURT (CONT'D)

The murders have all said something about the victims. A junkie given a fatal overdose, a cowboy hung with his own rope, a transvestite dying of crude castration, and a dipso dying of alcohol poisoning.

Pause.

RANCOURT (CONT'D)

We know all this – but why has he stopped killing clowns all of a sudden?

KAVANAGH

Maybe he's found his sense of humor and thinks they're funny *all of a sudden.*

Kavanagh is being sarcastic.

RANCOURT

Hang on – you are saying he killed the clowns because he didn't think they were funny? He killed them because they were bad clowns?

KAVANAGH

I was joking about him finding his sense of humor.

RANCOURT

So, he found the clowns irritating enough to kill them but now he doesn't?

KAVANAGH

Maybe he has just made his point and has quit while he's ahead? Maybe he's left town and started killing clowns some place else?

RANCOURT

No, the FBI would have told us if he was killing clowns in another city.

He's stopped because he's not pissed off with clowns right now.

Pause.

RANCOURT (CONT'D)

He killed clowns because they were bad clowns. Let's run with that idea.

KAVANAGH

You are saying that the killer is some master clown who has been offended by four inept street clowns, to the extent that he felt compelled to whack them?

RANCOURT

It's an idea. Is there a school for clowns? Is there such a thing as a Professor of clowning?

KAVANAGH

Yeah, he's called the Mayor.

Rancourt is deep in thought and ignores Kavanagh's quip.

RANCOURT

Some guy who takes clowning *so* seriously, that street "amateurs" drive him to murder.

KAVANAGH

So why stop, when there are so many inept clowns still out there?

RANCOURT

He must have other priorities right now. You're right, there's no shortage of crap clowns out there.

Rancourt points out to the street. Half a dozen clowns, in assorted costumes, walk past the bar.

KAVANAGH

It looks like we've started letting them out.

Kavanagh turns to his glass and drains his pint.

INT. EXPENSIVE FRENCH RESTAURANT. NEW ORLEANS.
NIGHT.

"Hulot" and Nancy are sharing a romantic candle lit dinner for
two, in an expensive restaurant that overlooks the city of New
Orleans - the couple only have eyes for each other. Nancy
looks stunning in a black evening dress; her hair tied in a
chignon. Hulot is wearing his usual buttoned up suit which is a
couple of sizes too small. He has dispensed with the pipe and
removed his hat for the occasion.

NANCY

This is lovely, Jacques.

Jacques nods in acknowledgement.

NANCY (CONT'D)

My first husband never took me anywhere as nice as this.

HULOT

Why not? Eez normal, no?

NANCY

I never thought I would date another foreigner again. No
offence Jacques, but the trouble I had with my ex husband.

Nancy shakes her head in mock exasperation.

HULOT

He was from Russia, you say?

NANCY

Yes, Moscow.

Pause.

71

NANCY (CONT'D)

That's where he is now, as far as I know. My lawyers are trying to track him down so he can sign the appropriate forms, and we can *finally* get divorced. The State of Louisiana does not recognize abandonment alone, as grounds for a legal divorce.

HULOT

Do you think there is any chance of a reconciliation, Nancy?

NANCY

Absolutely not.

Nancy reaches across the table to hold Hulot's hand.

NANCY

Besides, he cannot get back in The US – he was deported after he got out of prison.

HULOT

He sounds like a crazy man.

Nancy takes a sip of her wine.

NANCY

He is crazy. We hadn't been married long before his insane jealousy started to show itself.

HULOT

Ow so?

NANCY

I used to work in a bar in the French Quarter, and naturally you talk to a lot of people – it is part of the job. Ivor, that is his name, came in the bar one day as I was talking to a male customer. He went ballistic, accusing me of infidelity, and ended up hitting this poor guy who was just being friendly. I lost my job because of that incident, and Ivor ended up in prison for 6 months. Because he was here on a temporary work visa, they deported him to Russia on his release.

HULOT

Were you upset about that?

NANCY

No, by then I had decided to cut my losses. Ivor is a violent maniac. Who is to say that he wasn't going to turn his violence on me?

Hulot nods in agreement and smiles.

HULOT

You're right. You're better off without him.

Nancy nods.

NANCY

Now I'm trying to rebuild my life, and you are the first man I have been attracted to since Ivor. When you came in the café that day it was your courtesy and gentleness that draw me towards you – and you are a foreigner? Who would have thought?

Nancy giggles and Hulot laughs too.

HULOT

The worst eez behind you now. I will take care of you, ma Cherie.

The couple hold hands across the table and share a delicate kiss.

INT. MARIE LAVEAU BAR. FRENCH QUARTER. NEW
ORLEANS. NIGHT.

Kavanagh is seated at the bar alone, drinking whiskey. There is
a solitary bar tender who intermittently replenishes Kavanagh's
glass, with a fresh shot of booze. The detective looks lost in his
own thoughts. Rancourt enters and sits down on a stool next to
Kavanagh. On the wall behind the bar is a giant mural of the
famous voodoo Queen, Marie Laveau – the pub is named in
her honor.

Kavanagh nods at the mural.

KAVANAGH

We could do with some of her voodoo magic to find our clown
killer.

Rancourt does not respond to the remark.

RANCOURT

I figured you would be in here - thought I'd give you a heads up.
Rancourt takes out his police notebook and begins to read from
it. All small boat owners in Louisiana cross referenced with
known violent felons – we are talking anyone with a conviction
from bar brawling to murder - giving us 965 possible suspects
in total.

Pause.

RANCOURT (CONT'D)

Of that 965, 921 are white middle aged males. All of the 921
have been interviewed and checked for their whereabouts at
the times of the murders.

Pause.

RANCOURT (CONT'D)

Of the 921, 657 were out of state at the time of at least one of the murders and can verify they were not in Louisiana when stated absent. That leaves 264 possibles, 198 of whom can be rules out due to infirmity or lacking the physical strength to be our man. That leaves 66 possibles.

Pause.

RANCOURT (CONT'D)

59 of the remaining 66 have cast iron alibis for the times of the murders. The remaining 7 all live alone but have been interviewed at length by detectives, and none of them have committed a violent crime in the last 25 years. 5 of the 7 have been interviewed personally by us, and ruled out as possible suspects. The two remaining suspects that we did not personally interview, have since come up with alibis that check out. One was having an affair with a neighbour's wife, which he didn't want to own up to at first. The other guy was at an out of town brothel, confirmed by at least 3 hookers, on the night of The Super Dome murder, and couldn't logistically have perpetrated that crime.

Kavanagh is wearily shaking his head out of a sense of frustration. Rancourt changes the subject, putting his note book away.

RANCOURT (CONT'D)

I've been doing the rounds, talking to all the street clowns. It's as if the murders didn't take place – they are all back out there.

Rancourt nods towards the street.

RANCOURT (CONT'D)

I've asked them to be vigilant and report anything or anyone suspicious. Not that I think they were listening.

KAVANAGH

You want a drink?

RANCOURT

Yeah, why not? A red wine, please.

The bar tender has overheard and starts to pour a glass of red, which is then placed in front of Rancourt.

KAVANAGH

On my tab.

The bartender nods.

KAVANAGH (CONT'D)

It looks like they are going to take me off the case.

Kavanagh takes a slug of his whiskey.

RANCOURT

What makes you say that?

KAVANAGH

The Feds have been down to see the Chief and the Mayor in person.

RANCOURT

You know as well as I do that the Mayor is up for re-election, and if the clown killer could be caught then that would look good for him.

KAVANAGH

Yeah, I understand how City Hall works.

Pause.

KAVANAGH (CONT'D).

I really thought we'd have caught this son of a bitch by now. No one knows this city like us – least of all some hot shot Fed from Quantico.

Both detectives take a drink.

RANCOURT

C'mon Paddy. It's unlike you to get down over a case.

KAVANAGH

I'm taking this one personally, Rancourt. I don't like being made a fool of on my own patch. This clown killer is shafting us like a couple of bitches.

Pause.

RANCOURT

He'll be back, Lieutenant. He's building up to his big finale. Then we'll catch him.

KAVANAGH

Well, he better hurry up. At this rate, I won't be around.

Kavanagh raises his glass to the mural of Marie Laveau.

KAVANAGH (CONT'D)

To you lady! I need your help.

EXT. ALGIERS DISTRICT. NEW ORLEANS. DAY.

Shot of a residential street. The houses are single story detached wooden dwellings, in need of a coat of fresh paint. The area around one house is cordoned off with police incident tape. There are several patrol cars parked up and uniformed police officers are trying to keep a few members of the public back from the scene. An unmarked police car pulls up - Kavanagh & Rancourt alight from the vehicle. They walk over to the crime scene house.

INT. NANCY'S APARTMENT. ALGIERS. N.O.

The apartment is in a state of disarray, with tables and chairs overturned and a broken TV set in the corner. Forensics officers are dusting the room for prints and taking photographs of the scene, while Detective Joyce leads Kavanagh and Rancourt into an adjoining bedroom. Nancy the waitress is lying face up on the bed – she is clearly dead.

KAVANAGH

So what are we looking at here, Joyce?

JOYCE

It looks like a domestic murder. Neighbors called police to report a domestic disturbance in the early hours – there was a lot of shouting and screaming coming from this house. When officers arrived the husband opened the door and led them to his wife here - she was already dead.

Joyce produces his notebook and starts to read.

JOYCE (CONT'D)

According to I.D. found in her handbag and confirmation by the neighbors, she is a Nancy Sokolov, and worked as a waitress in a café in The Quarter. The husband, Ivor Sokolov, is a Russian illegal immigrant. He has confessed to strangling her in the heat of a marital argument.

Both Kavanagh and Rancourt move closer to the body, inspecting its positioning and the marks round the victim's neck, consistent with death by strangulation.

JOYCE (CONT'D)

Ivor Sokolov has been arrested and taken down the central police station.

Close up shot of the victim's face. She looks like she is asleep.

KAVANAGH

What a waste.

RANCOURT

It looks like we are back to senseless murder again, in all its banality.

KAVANAGH

Yeah, there's no clown killer involved here.

INT. KILLER CLOWN'S APARTMENT.NEW ORLEANS. NIGHT.

The killer, still dressed as "Hulot", is sat on the sofa watching the news on TV. The death of Nancy Sokolov is being reported. At first, the killer is paying no heed, and is occupied reading a newspaper. He casually glances at the screen as Nancy's photo comes up on the screen. Suddenly his facial expression turns to one of horror. Dropping the newspaper, he begins to wail.

The shot fades to black.

Shot of the killer seated at his dressing table. He is slugging whiskey from a bottle and weeping inconsolably.

The shot fades to black.

Shot of the killer smashing his room up with a baseball bat. He smashes the dressing table mirror. He attacks the mannequins with the bat. He collapses in a heap, his body shuddering with spasms of grief.

The shot fades to black.

Shot of the killer staring fixedly at the TV screen as an old silent movie of Charlie Chaplin is playing –the killer's facial expression is completely blank and devoid of all expression.

The shot fades to black.

EXT. BOURBON STREET. FRENCH QUARTER. NEW ORLEANS. DAY.

The French Quarter is packed with people, attracted by a Mardi-Gras parade. A variety of garish, techno-color floats are being driven along the street, to the delight of the massed tourist ranks. The floats are carrying giant *papier-mache* heads of grotesque proportions – the Queen of Hearts from Alice, toy soldiers, and Chinese dragons.

Shot of the killer's tear stained face as he weaves his way along the sidewalk, bumping into spectators unapologetically, as he goes. Unshaven and unkempt, the killer clown looks like a tramp.

EXT. JACKSON SQUARE. FRENCH QUARTER. NEW ORLEANS. EARLY EVENING.

"Macca", the silver metallic robot clown, is performing in the square. A small crowd of tourists has stopped to watch Macca go through his routine, which consists of a medley of statuesque poses, robotic mime, and for his *piece de resistance*, "Moon Walking". Macca has a box of lollipops which he distributes to kids, emotionally blackmailing the parents into tipping for the "gift". No parent wants to be seen as churlish or cheap in front of their smiling child, and other members of the attendant public. A tramp is stood at the front of the crowd, ironically jeering, as Macca plays the crowd.

KILLER CLOWN

Bravo!

It is not clear to Macca whether the "tramp" ("Killer Clown") is being ironic, though his applause and cheering are over the top. Macca is irritated by the tramp but continues to stay in character and keep quiet, while holding a motionless pose.

KILLER CLOWN

Bravo! Bravo! Encore! Encore!

There is a hostile tone to the "tramp's" applause.

One or two people in the crowd start to laugh, while others are moving off. Finally, Macca snaps out of character and feels compelled to say something.

MACCA

Listen buddy, I don't know what your problem is, but I'm trying to make a living here. Why don't you just fuck off!

KILLER CLOWN

A living? What is it exactly you do for a living?

MACCA

Oh you're funny, dude.

KILLER CLOWN

Which is more than I can say for you.

Again, there is some tittering in the crowd.

MACCA

You think you can do better?

KILLER CLOWN

As a matter of fact I do, but I have more pressing matters to attend to right now.

Pause.

KILLER CLOWN (CONT'D)

I couldn't help noticing your original take on the Moon Walk. Out of interest, who do you think started that dance move?

MACCA

Michael Jackson, right?

KILLER CLOWN

Wrong! It was a move created by tap dancer Bill Bailey in the 1950's, and originally called the "backslide". Jackson plagiarized it many years later, executing the move in a performance of "Billy Jean". Marcel Marseau used it throughout his career in his mime routine, "Walking against the Wind".

The tramp/Killer Clown performs the Marceau mime expertly. The crowd applaud.

MACCA

Listen buddy, that's very impressive, but I don't need no history lesson. Time is money as they say.

KILLER CLOWN

I'll pay for your time.

The tramp/Killer Clown throws a $50 bill in Macca's box.

KILLER CLOWN (CONT'D)

You haven't got much time left.

MACCA

What's that?

KILLER CLOWN

Your performance will soon be coming to a climax.

MACCA

You're right – I've had enough of your shit for one day.

Macca climbs down off his plinth and starts to empty the contents of the collection box into his pockets. He holds the $50 bill up to the tramp.

MACCA (CONT'D)

I'm going to *particularly* enjoy drinking this sucker away!

KILLER CLOWN

It saddens me that you are so motivated by money. Here take another $50.

The tramp throws a $50 bill at Macca, who doesn't hesitate to pick it up.

MACCA

Keep 'em coming asshole. I can take this kind of abuse all day.

KILLER CLOWN

You don't seem to realize that art should be practiced for art's sake; that clowning is the most noble of professions. You sir, do a disservice to the profession, which through the ages has been a critical voice against tyranny and the abuse of power.

MACCA

Yeah? Go blow yourself. How's that for satire?

By the way, tell me your dealer's name – you are on some impressive shit.

KILLER CLOWN

I gave you a chance to see the error of your ways.

The tramp/Killer Clown pulls an automatic pistol from his back pocket, taking aim at Macca. He fires off 6 rounds and kills Macca stone dead. There is a deathly silence in the crowd before a woman screams. The tramp casually starts to walk away up Decatur Street, in the direction of the casino. There is the distant sound of an approaching police car.

INT. KAVANAGH'S OFFICE. POLICE STATION. NEW
ORLEANS.

Kavanagh is sat at his desk studying paperwork relating to the
clown killings. Rancourt comes rushing into the office in a state
of high excitement.

RANCOURT

Let's go Lieutenant. The Killer Clown looks like he's struck
again. A robot clown has just been shot dead in Jackson
Square. The perp. was seen heading up Decatur in the
direction of the casino.

Kavanagh grabs his jacket and the two detectives run from the
office.

EXT. HARRAH'S CASINO. NEW ORLEANS. EARLY
EVENING.

"Alex", the silver metallic robot clown, is stood outside the
entrance to the casino. Some casino customers stop to give
Alex a buck. The tramp/Killer Clown approaches Alex.

INT. SQUAD CAR.

Shot of Rancourt at the wheel with Kavanagh in the passenger
seat. The vehicle is being driven at high speed through the
streets of New Orleans, with siren wailing. Kavanagh and
Rancourt are looking ahead trying to locate the tramp/Killer
Clown on the streets as they fly past.

Shot out of squad car from the passenger's perspective.
Façade of Harrah's casino. A tramp can be seen talking to a

silver metallic robot clown on the steps in front of the entrance to the casino.

Shot of Kavanagh and Rancourt in the squad car.

KAVANAGH

Look! There! Pull over.

Shot of the Squad car as it comes to a screeching halt. The two detectives jump out of the car with guns drawn. Kavanagh shouts at the tramp/Killer Clown.

KAVANAGH (CONT'D)

You! Drop your weapon and freeze. Get on the ground.

Shot of the tramp/Killer Clown as he turns to face Kavanagh, while grabbing the arm of Alex. The Killer Clown has a gun placed in Alex's back. The killer and his hostage start to back up into the casino as a crowd of Japanese tourists are leaving the casino lobby.

RANCOURT

Hold your fire Lieutenant.

Shot of Kavanagh and Rancourt - guns drawn at arm's length, the two detectives cautiously climb the steps, and follow the Killer plus hostage into the casino.

INT. HARRAH'S CASINO. NEW ORLEANS.

Shot of the casino's central aisle from the viewpoint of the main entrance. 100 yards in the distance, the Killer Clown has hold of Alex, and is making his way towards the riverside exit – Kavanagh and Rancourt are in pursuit. The Killer Clown turns and fires a couple of rounds in the direction of the detectives.

All hell breaks loose in the casino, with people diving for cover.

One of the bullets hits Rancourt in the leg - he goes down.

Kavanagh drags his colleague behind a slot machine and out of the line of fire.

Shot of Kavanagh crouched over Rancourt.

KAVANAGH

Are you okay Rene?

Rancourt smiles.

RANCOURT

What's with the Rene? Anybody would think we were friends.

Kavanagh reaches for his radio and speaks into it.

KAVANAGH

Officer down in the casino. Murder suspect is heading in the direction of the riverside. All units to the riverside, at the rear of the casino.

Kavanagh turns to Rancourt.

KAVANAGH (CONT'D)

Are you okay?

RANCOURT

It's just a leg wound – I'll be okay. You go get the bastard for me.

Kavanagh pats Rancourt on the shoulder and sets off at a run down the casino's central aisle. Members of the public are pointing Kavanagh in the direction of the killer's escape route.

EXT. RIVERSIDE. NEW ORLEANS. SUNSET.

The Killer Clown is dragging Alex down a flight of steps leading to a moored dinghy on the river. They both climb into the craft and the Killer Clown fires up the motor.

Shot of the dinghy pulling away from the river bank, just as Kavanagh is arriving at the scene.

Shot from Kavanagh's perspective as the dinghy motors away from the shore, now a 100 yards in the distance. Kavanagh considers shooting at the dinghy but decides against it. He speaks into his radio. As he does so police cars start arriving at the scene, with sirens blazing and lights flashing.

KAVANAGH

Kavanagh to all units. The murder suspect and hostage are in a dinghy and heading over to Algiers, in the direction of "Mardi Gras World". All units proceed to "Mardi Gras World". Repeat, all units proceed to "Mardi Gras World".

Kavanagh jumps into a police car, which careers off at high speed.

EXT. ALGIERS. NEW ORLEANS. NIGHT.

Shot of dinghy arriving at the Algiers side of the Mississipi. The Killer Clown and Alex climb out of the dinghy, and run/walk to the "Mardi Gras World" building – they enter, just as the first police cars screech to a halt nearby.

INT. MARDI GRAS WORLD. ALGIERS. NEW ORLEANS.

Shot of the interior of a giant warehouse full of Mardi Gras floats and Carnival paraphernalia. The giant *papier mache* heads and grotesque figures look sinister in the night light. The Killer Clown and his hostage hide behind one of the floats. The Killer Clown slugs Alex with the butt of his pistol rendering the hostage momentarily stunned.

KILLER CLOWN

Listen you prick, you give me any trouble and I'll blow your brains out. All I want you to do is sit quietly and don't try to escape.

The Killer Clown is taking in his surroundings in the dim light. He is sweating profusely and breathing heavily. Alex looks scared.

ALEX

Listen man – why don't you let me go? I don't even know you. Why are you doing this?

KILLER CLOWN

You don't get it, do you?

I'm the guy who has been eradicating all the clowns in town.

Alex now looks extremely scared – he starts to cry.

KILLER CLOWN (CONT'D)

Please, spare me the emotion. Your street performances have been devoid of emotion ever since you decided to denigrate the noble art of clowning. If only you had put your heart and soul into your work earlier.

EXT. OUTSIDE "MARDI GRAS WORLD". NIGHT.

Kavanagh's car has arrived at the scene, along with several other squad cars. Kavanagh gives Joyce his instructions.

89

KAVANAGH

Okay Joyce, make sure the area is completely sealed off and all exits from the building are blocked. I'm going in, to end this. If I need backup I'll radio for help.

JOYCE

Sir, you should wait for SWAT to arrive.

KAVANAGH

They might be too late. I think he's going to kill the hostage. Just do as I say, Joyce.

Before Joyce can reply, Kavanagh runs into the warehouse with gun drawn.

INT. "MARDI GRAS WORLD" WAREHOUSE. DARK.

The Killer Clown is crouched next to a dazed looking Alex. The killer starts to talk to his captive audience of one.

KILLER CLOWN

If only you had stuck to being the bum you, are and panhandled as a civilian tramp – I would have spared your worthless life. When you decided to sully the good name of clowning, you crossed the line, my friend.

Pause.

KILLER CLOWN (CONT'D)

Once you started to drag the legacy of the comic greats through the mud, then your fate was sealed.

Pause.

Shot of Alex shaking his head in denial.

Return to the face of the killer.

KILLER CLOWN (CONT'D)

Don't pretend you are a true clown dedicated to public performance; an educator and agitator standing up for the little man – a lampoonist of the pompous and the self righteous. You are a charlatan, sir – a talentless beggar and a hypocrite.

Shot of Kavanagh in a crouching position, searching the ranks of carnival floats, for the killer and his hostage. Kavanagh shouts to the killer.

KAVANAGH

Look, I know you are in here – the place is surrounded. Give up now and we can resolve this without further bloodshed.

Shot of Killer Clown's face. He hears Kavanagh's entreaty.

KILLER CLOWN

It's too late for all that copper.

Pause.

KILLER CLOWN (CONT'D)

You're the cop in charge – I recognize your voice from the TV appeal you made.

Shot of Kavanagh's face.

KAVANAGH

Yeah, I'm Kavanagh, Lieutenant Kavanagh – I'm in charge of the clown murders investigation. I'm here alone. I've come in to try and reason with you and resolve this situation. I think I understand you.

KILLER CLOWN

I don't think you *understand* me, Kavanagh. If you did, you would have caught me before now. You've only got this close to me, because I wanted it this way. Killing scum bag *clowns* was too easy- I got bored.

Shot of Kavangh's face. He is trying to locate the source of the killer's voice and silently edging in the perceived direction.

KAVANAGH

You're right – you were too clever for us. If you had stopped after number 4, we would never have caught you. What changed?

Shot of killer's face – he is starting to cry.

KILLER CLOWN

I lost the *only* person I have ever cared about. She was beautiful and pure, unlike this scum here.

Shot of the killer pointing the gun at Alex. Alex starts to plead for his life.

ALEX

Don't kill me man.

KILLER CLOWN

Why should I spare you, you sniveling drone? Whatever your name is?

ALEX

Alex, man.

KILLER CLOWN

Alex, short for Alexander?

ALEX

Yeah, man. My grandparents were Russian. They came to America to escape persecution.

KILLER CLOWN

The only person I have ever loved was killed by a *Russian*.

Shot of Kavanagh. He has his gun trained on the killer, who has his gun aimed at Alex. The killer suddenly notices that Kavanagh has him in his sights. The situation is reminiscent of a Mexican standoff.

KAVANAGH

What was the name of the girl you loved?

KILLER CLOWN

Nancy. Why, what's it to you?

KAVANAGH

Nancy Sokolov was killed by her Russian husband 2 days ago – here in Algiers.

Shot of killer's face. He looks shocked that Kavanagh knows the details of Nancy's death.

KAVANAGH (CONT'D)

We have the bastard who did it in custody – he will never see the light of day.

Pause.

KAVANAGH (CONT'D)

Is that why you stopped killing clowns? You fell in love with Nancy?

The killer nods and continues to weep.

KILLER CLOWN

She made me see the beauty in life. She made me forget all the ugliness.

The killer continues to point his gun threateningly at the trembling hostage.

KILLER CLOWN (CONT'D)

Before I met Nancy, I only saw beauty in art.

KAVANAGH

The art of killing?

KILLER CLOWN

The art of clowning. The killing was necessary in order to preserve the beauty of that art.

KAVANAGH

They were just bums trying to earn enough for a fix or a bottle of booze. What harm were they doing you, or the art of clowning?

KILLER CLOWN

I knew you wouldn't understand. You are a fool like the others. True clowns have exposed the follies of mankind throughout the ages. Through satire and mime they have drawn attention to man's greed and crass immorality. It is perverse for a clown's motive to be based on mere money and personal gratification; the very things that clowning should be attempting to ridicule and oppose.

KAVANAGH

You sound like a man who *has* plenty of money - idealists like you are all the same. You try to change the world for the *so called* better, not accepting that the world and the people in it will always be flawed and imperfect. You are a misguided dreamer.

Shot of the killer's enraged face.

KILLER CLOWN

Dreamer?

The killer turns to shoot Kavanagh. Kavanagh has anticipated the killer's movement. He fires repeatedly at the killer, who goes down.

Shot of Kavanagh's face.

KAVANAGH

Yeah, *dreamer*. And it's time you went to sleep, *for good*.

Shot of the silver hostage getting to his feet and fleeing the scene. Kavanagh is stood over the killer who is breathing his last breaths.

KAVANAGH (CONT'D)

You know what your problem was.

Pause. It is a rhetorical question.

KAVANAGH (CONT'D)

You took life too seriously. You should have lightened up.

Shot of the killer as he exhales his last breath. There is a hint of a smile on the killer's face as he closes his eyes for the last time. THE END.

Printed in Great Britain
by Amazon